Will T. Hale, Will T. (Will Thomas) Hale

An autumn lane and other poems

Will T. Hale, Will T. (Will Thomas) Hale

An autumn lane and other poems

ISBN/EAN: 9783337374662

Printed in Europe, USA, Canada, Australia, Japan

Cover: Foto ©Andreas Hilbeck / pixelio.de

More available books at **www.hansebooks.com**

AN AUTUMN LANE
AND OTHER POEMS

BY WILL T. HALE

NASHVILLE, TENN.   DALLAS, TEX.
PUBLISHING HOUSE M. E. CHURCH, SOUTH
BARBEE & SMITH, AGENTS
1899

TO DAVID RANKIN BARBEE

CONTENTS.

9

CONTENTS.

CONTENTS.

II

CONTENTS.

AN AUTUMN LANE.

I.

THE farthest hills that vaguely are outlined
    Are loveliest to the dreamer's pensive view;
The dearest years are those that lie behind,
    Far off and dim in recollection's blue.
I loiter, therefore, in the autumn lane
    That leads to where my earlier years were spent;
Old forms, old thoughts, old faiths come back again
    As all the past is with the present blent.
The dawn-gleams spread—soon will the car of light
    Pass yonder peak upon its world-long run:
Lo, out from Night's dark tunnel on the sight
    See the red headlight now, the rising sun!

II.

Beneath the glow that like a rapture springs,
    The frosted fields show an unwonted dress,
As though of down from visiting angels' wings
    Who passed above them in night's silentness.

Beyond the glistening runnel gray cliffs raise
    Heads that are ancient—turbaned in the blue—
As cities that were legends in the days
    When old Damascus flourished quaintly new.
Not here may come the sounds from where is whirled
    The city's smoke that all the welkin drapes—
Harsh hammerings on the anvil of the world
    Where rushed humanity its fortune shapes.

III.

Unvexed by much that makes the spirit sore
    With witnessing the war of Wrong and Right,
A peaceful stream that cheers a peaceful shore
    Day rolls between its banks of morn and night.
The upper waste, moved by nor winds nor tides,
    Spreads in calm beauty countless leagues away,
Where one cloud looms as if at anchor rides
    The Ship of Zion in some heavenly bay.
Within their wings a scrap of April sky,
    The watchful jays their strident warnings clang,
Where the low hills seem lonely mounds where lie
    The bones of giants from whom Anak sprang.

IV.

Here humble folk in humble ways have taught
  The truth too often now ignored by men:
Pure lives are echoes of God's holiest thought
  That sounds awhile betwixt the Now and Then;
Who for the sake of right have often done
  Some kindly deeds the world may never con—
White blocks of light they've quarried from the sun
  To form a stair to step to heaven on;
And proving, in their efforts to succeed
  Through shadows that envelop them, that still
That path is plain, in spite of night and need,
  That's lighted by the ruddy light, the will.

V.

Here likewise, as when Eve saw last the face
  Of her firstborn and dropped her trial tears,
Old Memory keeps her regretful gaze,
  And Love lives on, unaltered by the years.
The aged sit with their eyes turned Edenward,
  Where youth's flowers in perennial beauty show;
But though they would return, the decades guard
  With flaming sword the Gates of Long Ago;

15

While motherhood may sigh with quivering lips,
   Recalling some sweet child face known of yore,
"How dearer seem those on the outbound ships
   Than those who tarry with us on the shore!"

VI.

At noontide to the ears are wafted in
   Wind harmonies from out the minstrel trees,
Faint as we deem the distance-mellowed din
   Made by the wheels of passing centuries.
The insect-drones, continuous and forlorn,
   Out where the fallen leaves the moist earth press,
Hint of a fairy Samson grinding corn—
   Blind dupe of some Delilah's faithlessness.
The garrulous crows go flapping out of sight
   Where sumacs their ensanguined banners raise;
While on the fence a partridge stands upright
   And slides its whistle-shuttle through the haze.

VII.

Deep are the dyes of purple, gold, and green,
   And sweet all sounds the sylvan ways along;

Yea, all the earth is but a singing scene,
   And all the world is but a pictured song.
But distant are those joys my youth has known
   As things that now tradition only holds—
The trysts on twilight roofs of Babylon,
   And shepherd songs in Shinar's fields and wolds.
Old homestead! was it wisdom's part to choose
   A larger world and worldly views, in truth?
For taste Ambition's apple, and we lose
   The sweet faiths of the Paradise of Youth!

PRISCILLA.

THE untrod walks are still and dim,
　　And faint with hints of mignonette;
Upon the worn sundial's rim
　　Gray letters tell the motto yet:
I marke the time—butt Love doth notte,
　　Nor hathe since whenne the firste morn beamed;
And pathos hovers round the spot
　　Where fair Priscilla sat and dreamed.

I see her in quaint costume dight—
　　White-bosomed and with eyes of gray,
She looking down from girlhood's height
　　Far on the future's untried way.
What love songs here her days beguiled,
　　What poet was the most esteemed,
When her colonial lover smiled
　　Here where Priscilla sat and dreamed?

Perhaps the bosom now in dust
   Ached as she toyed some heliotrope,
And tears fell down as teardrops must
   When there is dearth of trust and hope.
But, coffined in the long ago,
   The breast that ached and eyes that beamed!
And Love *once* marked the time, I know,
   Here where Priscilla sat and dreamed.

A LAZY OLD DREAMER.

O NE of these lazy old dreamers?" I'll admit that's
 a pictur' of me,
Jest lollin' around in the suburbs—with a pole an' a
 line, it may be;
Or watchin' the peter-birds flyin' there over the still
 meader lands,
Or the God-woven scarfs of the alders, as white as a
 baby-saint's hands.

Fur away the *chug-chug* at the *de*pot of the injines in
 from a run,
Loud as Time, layin' down an' pantin' from the centuries' work he has done;
An' anear, the child-laughs in the orcha'd that have
 kept the old world fresh an' fair
Sence the fust little toddler in Eden thrilled the hearts
 of the earliest pair.

"One of these lazy old dreamers?"—I'll admit that the
    pictur' fits me—
But God wouldn't made all these beauties ef he never
    had wushed us to see;
An' I'm puttin' in time a-enjoyin' His handiwork
    morn, eve, an' noon,
By huggin' big arm-loads of summer an' gatherin'
    mouthfuls of June!

SILENCE.

DARKNESS and solitude! No harsh note falls,
Save when an owl, night's wary sentinel,
Cries out as hoarsely as the *All is well!*
Of some lone watcher sleepless on the walls
About a midnight city; the faint calls
Of fairies might be heard as here they tell
Love-secrets in their trysting; and the swell
Of wind chords faints and dies in Nature's halls.
Upon the upper desert yon cloud-swad
Seems the mirage of some great caravan,
And one half-deems the star worlds are anod
As their weak blinkings in the depths we scan:
The Silence is the chariot of God,
Whose spirit comes therein to plead with man.

THE CHILDREN.

WE hold the children's cherished hands
  To lead them through the years,
And as each tender mind expands
  We're filled with anxious fears.

But should we lose them—no more see
  The wee ones in the paths they've trod—
We'd learn *they* lead far more than *we*
  The way that winds to God.

VANITY.

I.

WE rail at our fate obscure, and sneer at the les-
sons of ages,
Where we chafe in the Valley of Peace and yearn
for the distant peak;
But we find at the last that the glow of the rainbow
but presages,
That the treasure we fain would grasp lies farther
the more we seek.
'Twere well could we realize the measureless distance
soon
Which spreads 'twixt our wishes and powers, however
Fame beckon and croon.

II.

We cherish ambition, and trust—whatever Content-
ment urges—
That pleasure will be the reward when striving is
over and done;

24

But up to the uttermost reach ring ever the earthly
    dirges,
  While clouds of regret at the top hang heavily round
    the sun.
And happier the one who learns, ere the difficult effort
    be made,
That thorns still last in the wreath long after the roses
    fade.

CONCEITED NEIGHBOR DICEY.

HE was just a singing master in an old-field singing
school,
And to blend his smiles with music was his most re-
deeming rule.

When the wondrous seven note book was the one in
general use,
He would pose in the revivals while his songs gushed
in a sluice!

With his right hand keeping time, he said this plainly
with his eyes:
"They must stir to beat our music with their harps in
Paradise!"

When the war of the rebellion rose between the States,
he wrote:
"I'm no theorist, Brother Lincoln, but I send in haste
this note:

When the fust great battle's comin,' let me march out
    to the front,
An' I'll warble 'Hail Columby' in the tones that I am
    wont.

Ef this fails to drive out hatred an' to make both sides
    ground arms,
Then I'll say for once I'm beaten and that music hath
    no charms."

So he went his way a-singing and believing in his
    soul
That his notes made earth more pleasant and they
    rang from pole to pole.

When he passed away he murmured: "I'm content
    to go up higher,
As the seraphs may be needin' of a leader for their
    choir."

And unless he changes greatly when among the saint-
    ly host,
He will spoil his first song service pausing now and
    then to boast!

But a truce to this amusement—did he lack in manly
part,
Cutting out the rubbish somewhat for the timid march
of Art?

Blazing pathways through our crudeness, let us name
him pioneer
Of the more advanced and classic with their notes of
sweeter cheer.

'Tis but justice to remember, when we'd criticise a
man,
That the acme of all honor is to do the best we
can.

GREAT SOULS.

I.

THE greatest spectacle of time
   Came when the curtain was uprolled,
Displaying there, so simple and sublime,
   One who across Judean vales had trod—
Who reaching high from Calvary with agony untold,
   Cast all the hopelessness of man down at the feet
     of God!

II.

Below, far under that stupendous plane,
   And yet, and yet sublime, it seems to me
   Some spirits still on earth there be,
     Alive unto the people's ruth—
Sent forth in one pathetic song—
Who stand again
   Before the Now's Thermopylæ;
     And, mailed in courage, clasping the keen truth,
Hold back the minions of old Wrong.

III.

Do such souls fail?   The end will prove
No battle's lost when it is moved by Love,
    Who hears the cry
    Of overawed humanity.
  So, whatsoever years may bring—
  A darker age to fling
  Its shadow o'er us, deep and dread;
  Or whether universal peace shall spread
Her sway the universe to span—
  From out the dust of the remotest days
  Will spring the flowers of his praise
Who feels the cause of Liberty's the cause of man!

A THANKSGIVING SONG.

THERE'RE some of us left yet, my dearie, from
    days that were passingly fair,
When home was a latter-day Eden and peace bur-
    geoned everywhere.
What mattered that Wealth, like the Levite, passed by
    on the farthermost side?
That home is the richest, I'm thinking, where Love
    and Contentment abide.
The little ones then were about us, and Joy sang its
    hopefulest strain,
And God in the cool of the daytime walked here on
    the earth once again!
Our table was long, and the pathos of lessening—
    leaf at a time—
Came only when both of us bordered the soberer days
    of our prime;
And somehow or other, my dearie, to-day tender mem-
    ories flow
To the Thanksgiving times that have faded—a long
    and a long time ago.

You mind how the boys came, my dearie, long after
  they'd wandered away,
To spend at the home of their childhood the dear and
  the hallowèd day?
The girls, too—long ago married—how gayly they
  passed the glad hours;
While we—yea, the present was brightened by bor-
  rowing the past's fragrant flowers.
Well, silly old man they may call me, who lingers too
  long in the past,
And over and over and over cites pleasures that never
  could last:
But ever and aye I am dreaming the change that is
  coming along,
All filled with the gleam of white pinions and sweet
  with the seraphim's song,
Will bring a reunion, my dearie—a Thanksgiving
  meeting, we know,
Far sweeter than any experienced a long and a long
  time ago.

THE EMBALMER.

YEA, an embalmer liveth still
    To save men's actions and their names;
And mummies in their wrappings fill
    The musty Catacombs of Fame.

The chieftains of the centuries—
    The great and true of eons long—
These will be shown to future eyes
    Through the preserving power of Song.

3   33

A VETERAN'S RECOLLECTION.

WHEN old Sherman marched," says he,
"Frum Atlanty to the sea,

Yankees hadn't much respec'
Fer us Rebels, recollec';

Burned our barns an' stables an'
Longed, I s'pose, to burn the lan';

Looted rich an' wronged the pore—
Till a crow'd starve, some one swore.

One day, though, a crowd of men
Went to raid a farmhouse, when

Suddenlike they in a room
On a little cradle come.

All about it crape wus tied,
Tellin' that a baby'd died.

Cap'n—as they called him—stood
Silent as a statyure would;

'Back,' says he, 'tetch nothin' here,'
An' he breshed away a tear.

I'm not lovin'—not a bit—
Them that Sherman had there, yit

Cap'n seemed to have a soul
All too tender fer control;

Should I meet him, certainly I'd
Shove all prejudice aside,

An' exten' a han','" says he,
"Fer the baby's memory."

WHEN THE QUAILS CALLED IN THE WHEAT.

THERE are never days as joyous as the childhood
    days at home,
And no spots so full of glory as the places where we'd
    roam;
Say within some wayside orchard, where their lace the
    spiders spun,
And the shade was an oasis in the desert of the sun;
And the green fields spread about us, and the blue
    fields spread above,
And the whisper of the leaflets was as low as mur-
    mured love;
While a rent was torn through silence when, from out
    their green retreat,
Pairing doves began their cooing, and the quails called
    in the wheat.

Why, to tarry by some streamlet was a glory for the
    sight,
As we watched the shoaling suckers flash like bars of
    splintered light;

There was concord in the singing of the farm hands
    in the vale;

There was cadence in the beating of the redhead's
    tiny flail;

Out among the clover blossoms or the grapevine's fra-
    grant glooms

Bee-hums sounded like a hymn that lingered tangled
    in the blooms;

And we had our childish fancies, saw our castles rise
    complete,

When the doves began their cooing and the quails
    called in the wheat.

Would that we could call back even one short day of
    all those days,

For a stroll about the meadows and the old familiar
    ways;

And while drinking in the beauty where the wild rose
    cheers the dawns

With the fragrance spilled from censers swinging on
    celestial lawns,

37

See an old form at the homestead, as her singing meets
our ear

In a voice whose music somehow is the dearest one
may hear!

And we half wish life had ended with the childhood
visions sweet,

When the doves began their cooing and the quails
called in the wheat.

CLARA BARTON IN ARMENIA.

THE world owes much to woman! Miriam's
songs
Cheered sweetly those who carried in their fates
The fetal Son who oped the guarded gates
Of heaven unto man; a nation's wrongs
Ended when Esther's love untied the thongs
That bound it; roar of cannons and the grates
Or dungeons have not awed her; and she waits
Near battlefields to soothe the weltering throngs.
But never yet hath worthier deed been done
Than hers, which braved the Islam where he stood,
Fed want, and brought to clouded lives some sun.
When wrinkled Time, in retrospective mood
Shall brood o'er past things, he will point to none
Nobler than her who did there "what she could."

"AL'AYS BEHIND."

WELL, Lem wus a caution, an' no mistake—
Al'ays behind, so 'at some one said
He'd be 'mongst the last of us all to wake
    When Gabriel should sound his trump fer the
        dead!
When he j'ined our regiment we made this fling:
"He should j'ine the immunes, ef anything;
He is fever-proof—fer certainly he's
Too slow to ketch any sort of disease!"

One day a squad of us regilers went
    In an ambush spread by our cunnin' foes;
An' then at the end of the gap arose
The yells of the heathen with volleys blent.
The few of us left prepared to run
To a place that would shelter—all 'cept one;
An' he with his smokin' carbine stood
    At the mouth of the gap, with his eyes of blue
    Ablaze with a light you'd liken to

Mixed fire an' devil an' thunder an' blood! . . .
An' Lem held the savages well at bay
   Fer full five minits, till his comrids found
   A chance to retreat to protected ground—
Left in the rear, as his custom, that day!

The captain cried when relatin' how
   The fellow had saved his remnant then;
An' as fer me, I'm ready to vow
   God knows His biz'ness more than us men.
While they's need fer the swift—they's times, you
    know,
When a feller's *right handy* in bein' slow;
An' we thanked Him fervently in our mind
Fer buildin' this man that wus "al'ays behind."

DO YOU CARE?

ALONE in my room in the twilight,
   With all so quiet, my ears
Catch the echo-ghosts of the whispers
   You spoke in the old glad years.
And I who swore that my soul no more
   Should yearn for a face that's fair,
Recall old days and their tender grace,
   And wonder if yet you care.

Do you ever, as I, hear the music
   Deemed sweet by you and by me,
In the tremulous light that never
   Shone yet on the land or sea?
That your breath lives yet in the mignonette,
   And your laugh in some fugitive air,
And the light of your eyes in the morning skies—
   Would you, knowing all this, yet care?

DO YOU CARE?

Might I clasp your hand in the silence
    Reached out o'er the desolate past!
Might I press one kiss on your forehead,
    Though the pleasure should be my last!
Heigh-ho! farewell to the dreams that dwell
    As ghosts in the gloom back there;
But I wish that I knew that your heart beats true,
    And if really you yet care.

BABY'S PRAYER.

IN looking backward now they come to me—
    The scene, the shadows, and the summer air,
His little head low bowed upon my knee
    As sweetly offered he his childish prayer:
"B'ess papa, an' my ma, an' all who need,
    An' make of me a dood boy, I am p'ayin'—
But if at firs', dear Dod, 'ou don't sutseed,
    Den 'twy, twy adain!"

I smiled—but on the smile there also went
    To God another simple prayer from me,
Repeated now with teardrops sadly blent,
    For the dear boy wherever he may be:
"If he should stumble in the untried way,
    Still plead with Thy dear Spirit from aloft;
Be patient should his feet be led to stray
    Not once, not once, but oft!"

THE WARNING OF TIME.

(On the Oppression of Finland.)

NOW look you, O rulers, and marvel!" came
   hoarsely the voice of old Time;
"Forget not that I am still watchful, being only to-
   day in my prime.

And listen: I've witnessed all movements that ever
   have cursed earth or blessed,
And I can compare all the epochs, and say which is
   worst, which is best.

I looked, in the far-off Beginning, as sweetly the
   morning stars sang,
And saw the Lord taming wild chaos, while cosmos
   to symmetry sprang.

I stood with my heart aching sorely, as I saw there
   in Eden one day,
Eve weeping in woe in the shadows, where the first
   of all murdered men lay;

45

Saw luxurious Greece's knees shaking as Alaric en-
    tered her home;
When Genseric came to Rome's borders, heard the
    chattering teeth of old Rome;

Watched the pleading and strangling of Poland as the
    robbers laid open her neck,
And Hungary's tearful entreaties as her nation was
    dashed into wreck;

While Freedom, like Sisera's mother, gazed long from
    her window dismayed,
And cried: 'Where is Liberty's chariots, and why is
    their coming delayed?'

Till I, who contrast all the eons and say which is best,
    which is worst,
May ask if, for all of our 'progress,' this age is as pure
    as the first? . . .

So remember that I am the Witness Jehovah relies
    on to tell
If the trusts placed in men are regarded, and if they
    be used ill or well;

46

And I shall prove ever unbiased till Deity the universe burn,
And His white hand shall scoop up its ashes, bestowing them safe in their urn!"

IN WINTER.

I.

A S some white captive who is forced to meet
A dusky lover, day moves on to greet
The night reluctantly; above the snow
An owl glides by as heavy as the flow
Of doubt through love dreams; in the cedar glade,
Made garrulous by the crows, a gory blade
Of sunset stabs the gloom; and faint and far
Comes sound of bells from where the glimmering
sheepfolds are.

II.

An ebon plaque with one blurred crimson rose—
Now from the copse a farmhouse window glows;
The moon, above a bare oak, limns below
A devilfish upon the spreading snow
With open arms; where in the summer wheeled
Shy doves, the corn shocks loom a tented field;
The light fades; silence; and then, faint and far,
The bells again out where the glimmering sheep-
folds are.

ORIGIN OF THANKSGIVING.

IN Scriptur' 'counts we l'arn dey lived sumwhah
    across de sea,
A man dat had a scap'g'ace son, as triflin' as could be.
He spent his days at circus shows, an' all his change
    per'aps
In fairo banks er try'n to win a fortune shootin' craps.

Dis chap wus called a prodigal—des what it means
    I'se sho'
I cain't explain—but dah he wus, true's two an' two
    make fo';
An' when his rocks give out he said he'd go back
    home ag'in,
An' see'f his pap would soften down an' let de wan-
    drah in.

De wimmin folks wus settin' roun' a readin' fashion
    books,
When down de tu'npike one young gal lif's up her
    eyes an' looks.

4   49

She says: "Heah comes dat hobo, pa—he's filthy, I
    declah!—
I'm glad my fellah is not close, to see him trampin'
    dah!"

But dat ol' man flung down his stick—went straight
    as he could go—
His long haih re'chin' down his back, an' wavin, white
    as snow.
"Do los' is foun' ag'in," he ses, between a sob an'
    laugh;
An' den, "I'll make de niggahs go an' kill de fatted
    ca'f!"

De hobo chased out to de branch, took out his bah
    ob soap,
And washes good; den kitchenwahd he stahted in a
    lope;
An' while he waited fo' de meal to cook, I tell you
    whut,
His stomic mighty nigh thought sho' de young man's
    th'oat wus cut!

"I'se hongry and can't wait," ses zee, "tell dat yere
    roast is done;
Ef dey is any possum cooked, or any brown co'n
    pone,
Or any ol' thing layin' roun', dess set it out," ses zee;
"Fer crum's f'om off de table now is good enough fo'
    me!"

Well, dey wus music in de yahd, and in de quahtahs,
    too,
De banjohs ringin' "Boom-de-ay," or "Linger Longer
    Lou;"
An' as de inst'uments rung out an' each his podnah'd
    swing,
I 'spec' de ol' man sasheyed out an' cut de pigeon
    wing!

I has no doubt about it, sah, Thanksgivin' stahted den,
An' it's been handed down each yeah to cheer de sons
    ob men; . . .
An' while I'se talkin' ob dese things, don't cah ef you
    would pass
A little ob de vittals, please, to break dis ol' man's
    fas'!

INDIAN SUMMER.

A SOLEMN stillness hangs o'er fields and woods
    As palpable as the blue veil that spreads
  About the world; one idle loiterer treads
On nuts that dam the stream; Red Riding Hoods,
The sumacs gleam amid the solitudes
  Where a shy woodchuck glides; the pitted heads
  Of thistles are wind shorn, and spiders' threads
Enlace the haunts where the gray sparhawk broods.
A faint pulsation, rings the cricket's beat
  Out in the grass where—gems of amethyst—
Protected gentians yet the eyesight greet;
  A sportive squirrel stirs the leaves; and hist!
A dove's voice in the haze—a symbol meet
  Of faith that calleth through death's shrouding mist.

A PETITION.

"But thou, when thou prayest, enter into thy closet."
(Matt. vi. 6.)

WHERE is this closet—in the solitude
 Where sylvan leaves with palpable soft stir
Seem to our ears the faint down-floating whir
From Time's wings as he flaps above the stream and
 wood?

What is this closet—shades of urban night,
Where o'er the revelry the coupling trains
Jar like the heavy noise of clanking chains
As Day (made captive), rousing, tries once more his
 might?

When I shall rest, with eyes that no more see—
Sadly alone when friends shall go their way—
Remember, Thou! one soul oft knelt to pray
Amid the solitudes of crowds and nights of revelry.

53

THE PREACHER.

LITTLE Bill, my boy, goes toddlin' round the
premises all day—
Jest a four-year-old, but havin' of an emperor's full
sway.

"Li Hung Chang"—we say—"from Chiny, never ast
more questions than
Little Bill, when he gits started fer to astin' questions,
can."

He will stop me fer a story when I'm busy in the fiel'—
Make me mend his trucks, er maybe pick a brier from
his heel;

An' it's strange I don't git worried—but I've changed
the last few years;
See more sunshine in the meaders an' more flowers
ever'wheres.

Somehow they is more of glory sneakin' round than
was of old,
While the world is full of music as the old world well
can hold.

54

"Guess some preacher's tetched your feelin's; you're
    a better man than once"—
Neighbors sometimes laugh an' tell me—"we can see
    sech differunce."

But I'm half of the opinion, silly as the words may
    sound,
Little Bill's the preacher done it as he goes a toddlin'
    round!

A TYPE AND AN APPLICATION.

OLD Colonel Dupont was a critic, an' he had a
kind word fer no one,

But he roasted some feller-man daily from his goods
box seat in the sun.

Pete Bond wus "a plug of a farmer;" Ike Blume wus
"no lawyer at all;"

Bill Higgins wus "sech a pore docter it's a wonder he'd
once got a call;"

An' ef he wus in all of their places he'd r'aly do some-
thin' or bust—-

When the fact is he'd never done nothin' but criticised,
whittled, an' cussed!

The world has a whole lot of colonels, an' them as
ain't colonels beside,

That foller his style an' ferever the failin's of others
deride.

You can count on this item as certain: that the one
that is quickest to blame

Is the feller that fell down the soonest in the race atter
    riches or fame;
An' every pore mortal that's risen knows well that
    the maxim is true,
That *talkin'* is easy as eatin', but *achievin'* is harder
    to do.

MARGARET.

SLIP of parchment, dim and old,
  Yet a tale it doth unfold:
"Farewell, Lover; you'll regret"—
This was all, and—"Margaret."

Yellow bit of gossip! for
Ninety years the escritoire
Hath its secret kept—and yet
I would know it, Margaret.

I can see the lovers now—
He hath curls about his brow—
Powdered; rings with rubies set
All his thoughts for Margaret.

She with garments of the flow
Of a century ago;
Sweet of disposition—yet
How your heart ached, Margaret!

53

MARGARET.

How your heart ached as you saw
Him some other beauty draw
In the reel or minuet—
While you flirted, Margaret!

For a lover's quarrel came
And you thought your passion's flame
Out; but then your eyes were wet,
Says this parchment, Margaret!

Fellow-feelings bind us; so
I am curious to know
If he ever felt regret?
Well, I hope so, Margaret.

A DREAM OF SPRING.

TO see the spring come in with pomp again!
    The dandelions like Circassians lift
  Black eyes to meet you; in the dampened rift
Of rotted leaves, the violets are fain
To stir from where all winter they have lain;
  Beside the fence the sorrel's mingled drift;
  While o'er the fresh-plowed furrows, flying swift,
The bluebird mocks the humming of the swain.
The sun, as one who for a time bemoaned
  His dead, smiles with a semblance of the joy
He felt ere summer died, once more enthroned;
  And zephyrs laugh the laughter of a boy
For spring, when God stoops and with potent breath
The earth from its long slumber quickeneth.

CHRISTMAS BELLS.

YEARNING wistful through the distance, long-
    lost comrades of the Past,
As the Christmas nears I hail you in a love that's still
    steadfast.
For last night I dreamed my footsteps had again
    strayed back to you,
And you met me with your smiles as ever you were
    wont to do.
Out above the brooding hills I saw the red streaks of
    the morn,
Like rose-bordered paths to heaven from a wilderness
    forlorn ;
In the village streets I lingered where as children we
    had played,
When we thought the hilltops bounded all the world
    that God had made ;
And we grasped and clasped a moment as before there
    came farewells,
      While we heard
        The bells a ringing—
          Heard the gladsome Christmas bells.

Long-hushed voices, dear old comrades, that within
    my dream would rise,
Sounded as though born of music drifting down from
    Paradise;
Thoughts of early sweethearts' greetings in the glad
    old-fashioned way
Brought some tears for dreams that perished in our
    youthhood's flowered May;
Friends who'd suffered seemed drawn closer unto me
    than they had been,
For the hearts that have their sorrows temper judg-
    ment on all men;
As about gone days we chatted and among changed
    ways we trod,
Earth seemed really drawn up somehow just a little
    nearer God. . . .
And I'd like to be in person where each old-time com-
    rade dwells,
        While the Lord's
          Good will's a ringing
            In the gladsome Christmas bells.

THE BRIDGE.

I.

THE night and solitude their vigils keep,
   While the old world in sheets of moonlight
      lies,
   Her wrinkled face turned upward to the skies,
'The droning winds her murmurings in sleep.

II.

Then, lo! a bridge spreads, brightening evermore,
   In splendid arches on its piers of prayer;
   And with sure step I pass along to where
This bridge of faith juts on the Beulah shore.

THE DRESS.

HOW faded now—drawn from its place
   Where it hath lain for, lo, how longe;
But inne its wrinkled foldes and lace
   Live Aprile's scente and Aprile's songe.
I half-waye wonder if—bedighte
   Inne spotless robes onne yon far shore—
Shee is as winsome, pleasing, quite,
   As inne this lyttle dresse shee wore.

I see her inne ye olde wise, whiles
   Ye daintie, ribboned thing shee tries—
Rare roses inne her maiden smiles,
   Sweete poems inne her girlish eyes.
And what if, inne ye love I beare
   For ye deare one God gave of yore,
I deemed her but some angel's prayer
   Whenas this lyttle dresse shee wore!

64

Shee faded younge and left life dreare,
  Though sunshine came againe, forsoothe;
And inne mine age it seemes more near
  To where shee is than back to youthe.
And since my footsteps draw nigh where
  Shee waites—I thanke the goode Lorde o'er
That I shall greete her still as faire
  As when this lyttle dresse shee wore.

A SONG OF PATRIOTISM.
(The Spanish-American War.)

I HEAR a cry that rises and swells on every breeze,
No laggards on the shore and no laggards on the
seas;
From homes of Lee and Lincoln the patriot souls are
seen—
Thank God! the land's united, the old flag waves
serene!

Because she is long patient, let none dare go too far—
America, peace-loving, is not afraid of war;
And those of yore who wronged her have aye had
cause to weep—
Found every son a hero "and not a knight asleep."

Not vain the fire of Henry; not vain Revere's wild
ride;
Not vain the brave battalions who for their country
died:
From homes of Lee and Lincoln the patriot souls are
seen—
Thank God! the land's united, the old flag waves
serene!

THE LETTER.

RUMMAGING through a trunk well worn
    I come at last on a faded note.
What is the trifle, musty and torn?
    Ah, the letter that Asa wrote.

"I love you now, and shall ever love,
    Unchanged in life, and unchanged in death."
These foolish things it is filled full of,
    And the letter only lingereth.

It was written after a quarrel was through,
    And the sweet make-up that the lovers know;
And he thought it all, and I thought it too,
    A long and a long ago.

Time conquereth love, the cynic allows,
    And so say I the results denote;
But why a sigh over Asa's vows,
    And the letter that Asa wrote?

INHUMANITY.

OLD Mason had a boy went wrong,
   An Neighbor Beers he ups an' says:
"It's but a bad streak som'ers, pison-strong,
Fer parents' former sins, I guess."

Then Beers' son in a few short years—
Why, he turned out about as bad;
"But 'tain't heredity," this time says Beers;
"It's the bad company he had."

When there's—instid of charity—
This cruelty that flays and flogs,
I think, too, that the more sech men I see,
The more I reverence common dogs!

THRENODY.

I.

THE same deep sky and twilight,
   The same old hills austere;
But eyes that once were my light,
   Their presence is not near.

II.

The whippocrwill calls tender
   To night that nearer draws,
And the mute spiders render
   Their silent songs in gauze.

III.

And now, while stars are keeping
   Their watch on sea and shore,
Pale Memory pauses weeping
   Where two shall meet no more.

IT MAY BE.

IT may be sometime, when my patient face
   Is absent from the old familiar place,
You will recall with softened heart at last
How one hath loved you with a love steadfast;
And then shall I be paid for hope deferred,
The **never-coming** love glance and the yearned-for
     word.

It may be sometime when my hands are cold,
You then will miss the tender clasp of old.
I would not have you sad; but were this so,
'Twould be a comfort could my spirit know;
It could atone for all the barren past—
To know with death I **bought** one tender thought at
     last.

A SCIENTIFIC QUESTION.

SENCE I l'ahn'ed ter read de Bible I has put in
    plenty work
        Settin' roun' an' 'sputin';
No subject dat's respectible I'se ever tried to shirk,
        Settin' roun' an' 'sputin'.
But in all ob my experunce I'se nebbah got so nigh
Outen somepin' foh to argy an' ter spout erbout dat I
Had ter 'sert dat man's fo'fathuh wus a monkey, by
    de by—
        Settin' roun' an' 'sputin'.

An' I think it is my duty dat I rendah in ol' age,
        Settin' roun' an' 'sputin',
A little clinchin' question foh de layman an' de sage,
        Settin' roun' an' 'sputin':
Ef de monkey wus man's daddy, why'd he stop so long
    ergo
Havin' fokeses foh his chilluns, I would sortuh lak to
    know?
While de *scientists* may 'splain it, still I'se ruthuh
    stumped foh sho',
        Settin' roun' an' 'sputin'!

71

THE SNOW.

A MUDDY inland sea, the sage grass stirs
In undulations to the wind; the rill
Moans in the agony of winter's chill;
Within the woods hide ghostly whisperers—
Stilled when the startled quails with noisy whirs
  Seek safety in a copse; with neighings shrill,
  A stray horse wanders on a darkling hill,
Browsing among the mullein and dead burs.

When twilight dieth, softly flakes descend,
  As thistledown; an eagre-driven bark,
An owl's form sweeps across the gray, to blend
  With the black line of trees; and then the dark.
Night passes on, as pass the years, and, lo!
The badge of age on nature's head—the snow.

72

THE LITTLE PORTRAIT.

HEY, little boy in the red plush frame, alone on
    the mantel there,
You've the same sweet smile that we knew so well
    when the future spread out fair!
Little bright eyes with the ambushed smiles, innocent,
    blue, and true,
The time has been long, been long, my boy, since last
    we have looked on you;
Is it well with you now in the life you lead, in the
    Somewhere lying far?
For the old folks pray, as they've always prayed, God
    love you wherever you are!

Hey, little boy in your fadeless garb, and safe in your
    red plush frame,
There's never an unkind thought in our hearts; for
    you not a word of blame;

The shadows are thicker within the rooms, and deeper
    within our breast;
May they never once lengthen across your path, or
    cause you any unrest!
Through the nights and the days be sure, my boy, in
    the Somewhere lying far,
The same old prayer is our prayer always: God love
    you wherever you are!

THE DIFFERENCE.

COLUMBUS de Blank wus a tasty old chump
    As you'd find—well, in most any nation or
  State.
"Be modest," he said; "never sound your own
    trump;
  Repeating a compliment's not delicate."
He used to throw down Colonel Long's *Weekly
    Dirk*—
  "It makes one so tired, very tired," he would say;
"He copies what So-and-So says of his work—
  How a sense of what's tasty should wander his
    way!"

Soon Columbus de Blank bought a plant and begun
  For to write paragraphs in a ringing way, too.
When the *Journal* or *Blast* complimented his fun
  And his logical leaders, now what did he do?
Then to clip was appropriate—never once bored;
  He watched for the puffs, which he printed with
    zeal;
For it not only matters as to whose ox is gored,
  But whose vanity's touched, as to how we may
    feel!

75

A TRACKLESS TERRITORY.

NO harsher note sounds there than turtles' call,
    There all things are the same from day to day;
The minutes drop from time as petals fall
  From off the rose to wither and decay.

Thereward the prow of every ship is turned,
  And thereward are our fondest glances sent;
And yet no one, however he has yearned,
  Has reached the far-off region of Content.

A BOUQUET OF OLD RED ROSES.

SEEMS like recollection somehow seeks the days
    when it is rainin'
  Fer to send our fancy back'ard to the years that
    used to be;
An' a person sees the bygone with no effort much of
    strainin',
  That it does us good to look at even in the memory.
So that at this very minute I can plainly see an' smell
The bouquet of old red roses that my mother loved so
    well.

Soon as April sun an' showers set the flowers all to
    smilin',
  Then the yard wuz sweet with music of the dronin'
    honeybees;
When we'd trudge from work to dinner, there wuz
    nothin' more beguilin'
  Or suggestin' to a mortal of a land of peace an' ease,

Than to set down by the winder fer a moment's restin'
    spell,
Nigh the plain bouquet of roses that my mother loved
    so well.

Lookin' out on summer evenin's where the killdees
    wuz a cryin',
    An' the moonbeams seemed reflections of the ser-
      aphs' arms re'ched down,
Ef my boyish soul felt lonely over thoughts that set
    one sighin',
    Wuzn't she a-near to comfort an' to drive away
      care's frown,
As she sung some old-time anthem in the candlelight
    that fell
On the sweet bouquet of roses that my mother loved
    so well?

It might seem right quare and silly—but while think-
    in' of the hours
    In our home when she wuz livin' an' when I wuz
    jest a boy—

Should I be at last so favored as to re'ch the land
    where flowers
  Grow in never-fadin' beauty, an' there's nothin' else
    but joy,
Heaven would be sweeter holdin', where the angels'
    voices swell,
A bouquet of old red roses like my mother loved so
    well.

EXPERIENCE.

BEEN livin' sometime in a quiet sort of way,
But somehow I've gathered a proverb or two:
Ef you'd save yourself trouble, I'd jest caution you,
Don't hear all the things that the other folks say.

Been livin' as well as a pore worm could live,
With a heart purty free frum annoyance each day:
Ef you think that is well, then reguard what I say,
Don't see all the slights that the other folks give.

NATURE'S THEATER.

THE autumn prepares a spectacular show
    To the myriad spheres that are huddled in
    space;
Hidden hands turn slowly the star jets low,
  While full on the stage looks every face.

The curtain of darkness at last is uprolled,
  And the calcium lights of the dawn flush the
    lands;
Lo, the earth, in her beauty of green, red, and gold,
  And the wind-roar, as far-away clapping of hands!

MOONRISE.

LIKE moving figures in a dream,
  The cattle near the milking gap;
Dark as a passing evil thought,
  An owl flits by with noiseless flap.

And then a fair-faced Amazon
  Strides up the east, and soon has hurled
A thousand silver javelins down
  To drive the shadows from the world!

LOOKING BACKWARD.

A FLECK of the sun, or the balmy air
　　Jest off of the clover som'ers,
An' I pause at my work, and my thoughts go where
　　Fields sound to the spring's fust comers;
The bees in the dogwood blooms, an' the birds
　　Fresh out o' their winter qua'ters,
An' the shitepoke down where the browsin' herds
　　Draw nigh to the swishin' waters.

I re'ch my hand till I seem to grasp
　　The hands of the old-time fellers;
Growed dearer now they're beyond my clasp,
　　For nothin' like absence mellers.
Tom Jones, Jim Fite, the Starkses an' Kings,
　　Ef you knowed how much I hunger
To talk of nothin' but the old, old things
　　We talked of when we wus younger!

83

Say, what of the blue and shadery hills,
   Ridge-backed like to camels kneelin'?
An' what of the lane an' the whippo'wills,
   And the wild rose scents out-stealin'?
What's become of the Givans guirls, an' what
   Has become of the other lasses—
All holier now for days that are not,
   But asleep under Change's grasses?

The thoughts of youth should be left to the young?
   Let winter fergit there is roses?
Let the songs once sung remain unsung?—
   We plan, but *Regret* disposes!
An' comrids back there, I somehow wush
   I knowed you'd sometimes remember
In the toils of day or the twilight's hush, . . .
   What, cryin'? . . . Old silly December!

AS THE SUN GOES DOWN.

THE lonely old people—of what do they think
On evenings calm as the sun goes down? . . .
(As softly, white hair, as a hand from the brink
Of the unseen realms tender winds lift you,
And kiss you like friends that are always true
No matter if destiny love you or frown.)
From chairs where they sit in the warm summer air,
It is easy, I know, for the old eyes to reach
And rest their dim sight on the heavenly beach,
As to rest on the past over gray wastes where
There were beauty and youth and fame's sought
crown—
As the sun goes down,
As the sun goes down.

Ah, the wonderful change that behind them sweeps
On evenings red as the sun goes down—
Their childhood and manhood and wifely songs,
Ere Hope was bounden in Failure's thongs,
Ere the heart fell dismayed for its yearning leaps,

And age had forgot there was ever renown!
But looking ahead there's a view that falls,
   A glint of white sails on a far-away shore,
   The bloom on the faces that fades no more,
And the petals of roses on the jasper walls
     Extending their blush to the world old and brown—
         As the sun goes down,
         As the sun goes down.

UNCLE BILL'S LETTER.

WE had a note the other day from Uncle Bill, out
    West;
Been gone some twenty year or more, an' is by riches
    blessed.
He sent his photergraph along, an' in his letter said
He's livin' on the ranch alone, an' never yit has wed.
I guess the Maynard guirl still lives," he wrote, "an's
    purty still—
She who wus knowed as Roxey when I wus simply
    Bill?"

We showed the photergraph to her; she read the letter
    through;
An' with a little sigh she said—a little nervous, too:
"Well, Mr. Smith deserves good luck—a noble heart,
    God knows!"
An' then her face turned strangely pale—a white and
    withered rose.

87

Perhaps the kind words tetched a chord that straight-
like felt a thrill—
"She who wus knowed as Roxey when I wus simply
Bill."

They's undercurrents in all lives! . . . Around
her children play;
She has a husband who is kind—an' yit who knows,
that day
When she remembered that one heart in all the world
of care
Still turned to her in thoughtfulness and guessed her
pale cheeks fair,
She felt a feelin' of regret—thought of the dead dream
still—
When one wus simply Roxey an' one her lover Bill?

JOHN HOWARD PAYNE.

HE sang a simple chanson
   In those forgotten years;
The harsh world then grew silent,
   Then trembled into tears.
And still the tears keep falling,
   And still where'er men roam,
They bless again John Howard Payne,
   Who sang the song of home.

O one-time strolling poet!
   How calm must be your rest,
Where Memory's red roses
   Grow always on your breast!
And o'er the dust of cycles
   Time's loving voice will come
In deathless strain, John Howard Payne,
   For you who sang of home.

OLD JIMMY GRIFFIN.

OLD Jimmy Griffin! I see him now,
    Sun on his face and the snow on his brow,
Doddering about in his truck patch—fat,
And in blue cotton pants and plain straw hat;
Or lounging at ease in his rocking-chair
In the old-time porch with its cozy air,
The gourd vines climbing about the door
And the hollyhock blooms in the yard before.

"Evil thoughts may enter all minds," he'd say;
"Needn't hand 'em a chair, though, an' ax 'em to stay!
I've little edication, as any may see;
But my Bible's in English, an' plain to me.
It teaches some truths—take this with the rest:
Love God an' your neighbor an' do your best."
If we heed his advice, I guess that the Lord
Won't test us on grammar to give His reward!

PETRARCH'S LAURA.

(1327-1899.)

FIVE centuries and over
    Of joys and woes
Since Petrarch was her lover—
    The Provence Rose.

What must have been his passion
    That still it blooms,
While nation after nation
    Sink in their tombs!

Though cycles long have glided
    Into the past,
We know her truth abided
    His passion's blast.

And more than Love's high praises
    Is Virtue's fame,
That spurned to let shame's traces
    Smirch wifehood's name.

NIGHT VOICES.

THE night, as day, hath voices speaking loud
    The feelings of the Universe's heart.
  Though hushed the jarring turmoil in the mart,
The wild applause, the shouting of the crowd
O'er Cæsar raised or luckless Pompey bowed—
    There are sounds as of colliding spheres; you start
    To almost hear a swishing comet dart
Through stars that tremble at the wraith, flame-
      browed!
And then, through fields of space, where old Time stirs
    'Mong upper worlds as one with moistened eye
Pausing by fallen tombstones and so peers
    For some loved name, there echoeth a cry,
The loudest, though Jehovah only hears:
    The million-tongued protest of Misery.

ROBERT E. LEE.

In his book Gen. Longstreet criticises Gen. Lee.—News Item.

GIRT in his patriotism, and his shield
    That courage which the noblest Spartan knew,
He did what skill and valor on the field—
    When faced by sheerest Might—can only do:
    Destroyed for years War's marshaled hosts, and slew
Till nations wondered when such numbers reeled
    Before the prowess of the Southron true!
And those who, when the tocsin rang, appealed
To him to lead—no jot of love will ever yield.

All efforts of all men must ever be
    As vain as waves to quench the sun's fierce flame—
Though splashed by all the monsters of the sea—
    When bent to wrong the Chief's unsullied fame,
    Or tarnish that undying hero's name!
Old Time himself hath written this decree,
    Which none may change with good or evil aim:
"Safe in the people's admiration, we
Shall see no brighter halo than surrounds our Lee."

93

MY BROTHER.

A COUNTRY graveyard, and a long mound lone-
ly lying
Beneath the skies on cloudy days and fair;
And there you rest.   Love for some years will moan,
Then stranger eyes, your moss-grown name espy-
ing,
Will turn away—not knowing you, how should they
care?

Can God forget, though?   Then, so long as God re-
members
The hearts that followed Honor, veering not—
The hearts that loved Right for Right's sake alone—
Through all Time's Junes and through all Time's
Decembers,
Dear unambitious dust! you will not be forgot.

FAILURE.

I SAW him in his life's young years
   Bid Love farewell—sweet Love in tears :
"And what," I asked, "dost thou most prize?"
"Success," he said with laughing eyes.

I saw him after he'd grown old,
And fame was his—friends manifold :
"Thy heart," I asked, "for naught now sighs?"
"Yea, *Love*," he said with weary eyes.

THE CONDUCTOR'S WIFE.

I.

GENTLE Dolores, I thank you! A lingering
relict am I,

Ready to yield my life, anxious to say good-by.

Lonely, as well as I'm ill? Aching for some kind
word?

Since Allen first went away, but few sweet words have
I heard;

Not that my neighbors anear have proven the least
unkind,

And not that they through the days have been to my
sorrow blind;

But hearts that have known Love's tone but slowly to
tame ones take;

And you, you have sorrowed, I hear, knowing of tears
and heartbreak.

II.

I know if he'd had his will, he'd have come back to
me that day,

Forgetting the words that I spoke—and the cruelest
    words were they;
Sorrow had been unknown, but cleared as the sun-
    kissed brook,
True Love is so quick to forgive, so ready to over-
    look!
Something you've heard of the lie causing me many a
    tear,
But all of it, all of it yet has burdened no human ear:
Laid in the tomb of my heart, a putrid corpse in the
    gloom,
Cold as the form of Lazarus, four days dead in the
    tomb,
With never an interested one to enter and say:
    "Arise!
The fault was great, and yet not pardonless in God's
    eyes."

III.

Shall I tell it to you? I must, for, under the spell of
    disease,
My life's surely passing away, a leaf on a wintery
    breeze!

Married for more than a year, blessed with a baby's
    smile—
A talisman sent from Heaven to keep both our hearts
    from guile—
I thought Allen tired of me, my fretting and words
    of blame,
For I, you remember, was weak from the day our
    baby came.
And so one evening I saw, as plain as I see you there,
A woman clasped in his arms, and he called her young
    and fair.
He'd come on the eight o'clock train, and after a
    while with me,
Had hurried away to a friend he'd promised that hour
    to see.

IV.

Jealous? Of course! for I knew that virtue, however
    dear,
With men is not safe as with wives, guarded by love
    and by fear;
For the sins of a husband the curse is never so great as
    is ours—

A hell of contempt and of scorn, scorching Hope's
sturdiest flowers.
Our thoughts are but whispers of God, or else of the
evil one,
And 'tis ours to hearken to God's, and the other's sug-
gestions to shun.
And the night was a June night and clear, even down
there in the streets,
Where the smoke of the restless trains the eyes and
the nostrils greets—
A monster apoise and dark, apoise on its mammoth
wings
Over a world not fair, however the poet sings!
And I said: "I wish that the train that bore you home
to-night
Had brought you in but a corpse for treating my
constancy light;
Killing affection for aye, I wish they had tolled your
knell—
The long, long whistle at eight, and the clanging call
of the bell!"

V.

Morning time dawned at last, but night was never
    more dark:

When faith is slain in the breast, who heedeth the lay
    of the lark?

How dim fell the sun on the street now loud with the
    hawker's cry:

How desolate the little yard where the butterflies idled
    by!

He said he'd explain some day, and he worshiped me
    more than all,

And trust him and love and the truth, and away would
    fade doubt's pall.

But cruelly harsh and sore, never a kiss I gave—

Never a kiss or a glance to lighten his ride to the
    grave!

And kissing the babe, he said: "Ere father returns
    again,

Soften your mother's heart till it trembles to sympa-
    thy's strain."

He waved back his kisses to me, and one to the baby
    there,

Then went to the train with no kiss save that of the
morning air.

VI.

Ere the day had passed to the night I regretted the
words I said,
And I longed for the whistle and bell, and the glow
that the headlight shed.
I went to the cottage gate, and I looked with an anxious eye
Up, up the narrowing rails that jutted, it seemed, on
the sky.
But after a while my heart sank down in its weight of
fears,
For the cries from a ruined wreck came throbbing
within my ears :
And a flagman's voice told out, as over the yards he
crossed,
The train had gone through a bridge, and every soul
was lost!

VII.

He said he'd explain some day ; ah, Allen, the secret's
known!

'Twas his sister there in the dark who shared my affection's throne:

A sister who'd listened the tempter, listened in trust
and fell,

While he, with a brotherly love, sought to hold her yet
from hell.

Through the ten long years that have passed my heart
has longed for him,

Cried for a word or a kiss out of the silence dim;

And never a June night's passed I've not stood there
in the door,

Watching the eight o'clock train, on schedule time
as before,

While the hawkmoths rustled the vines, and the
switching cars moved slow,

And electric lights flashed out on the sullen river below.

VIII.

But the end of the waiting's here, and a blissful hour
to me!

Dolores, gentle Dolores, who knows but his face I'll
see!

Your hand but a moment, raise; tell to me what is that
    I hear—
The jar of great wheels rolling, coming ever and ever
    near?
Joy and his love once more! and, tolling Despair's
    wild knell,
One long, long whistle at eight, and the—clanging—
    call—of the—bell!

WHEN THE SNOW COMES DOWN.

DREAMING in the shadows,
　　Beside the smoldering fire;
And spirits and things earthly
　　Grow gradually nigher.
And thought will somehow, somehow,
　　Go outward from the town,
To where the dead are sleeping—
　　When the snow comes down.

How fare out in God's Acre
　　The dead wrapped in their shrouds—
The babes and parents sleeping,
　　Forgotten by the crowds?
The flying flakes are roses
　　That brighten the tombs' frown—
White roses God is scattering
　　When the snow comes down.

IN THE LIBRARY.

A RRANGED in shelves the thoughts are seen
      Of two who struggled long ago:
Keats charms yet—Keats of gentle mien—
   And Byron, how his numbers flow!
There was a tamer time we know
   When men decried their power and fire;
But for those souls' rhymed overflow,
   A million readers now admire.

Ah, beauties yet lie hid, to be
   Revealed to future skeptics' eyes;
Truths Shakespeare, even, did not see
   Shall win the praises of the wise.
And scoffers may deplore with sighs—
   As those of old—"our common clay,"
But cycles hence the crowd will prize
   Some slighted toiler of to-day.

105

IF WE HAD KNOWN.

IF we had known
The murmurs coming from unheeded lips
Had been the last before the eyes' eclipse,
And the warm clasping of the living hand
The last ere hidden in the Silent Land,
We would have lingered longer, longer there
Where doom was crouched within the brooding
   air,
      If we had known.

If we had known!
We realize there's but a step from day
To that drear realm wherein the shadows stay,
And sweetest laughter from the heart, joy-flushed,
Can the next moment be forever hushed;
And yet somehow we carelessly forget,
Till forced to cry in wild and vain regret—
      If we had known!

SAYING GOOD-BY.

JUST a kiss, a sigh, good-by—
    This for us at summer's ending.
Are we happier, you and I,
    For the hours we've been spending?
Sweetheart! happier, you and I,
        Saying good-by?

Just a few weeks' pleasant talks,
    Sweet with eglantine and clover;
But recalling tryst and walks,
    Would we mind to live them over?
Sweetheart! would we, you and I,
        Saying good-by?

VALENTINE DAYS.

THE custom was a simple one, and filled with pleas-
ure, too,
  When we were young, my friend, when we were
    young;
And have we known of sweeter times, or hearts that
    beat as true,
  Since we were young, my friend, since we were
    young?
On the inside or the outside of the plain, old-fashioned
    home,
The lights of heaven shone about from morning till
    the gloam;
If care gleamed, 'twas as far away as was some feeble
    star
That twinkled but as sun-kissed sand upon a distant
    bar.
A realm of fragrant roses, and a kneeling at Love's
    shrines—
Those faded days when 'mong old ways we thought of
    valentines.

We've long since given up the things that made us
    happy then,
  When we were young, my friend, when we were
    young;
The manlier duties of the world must satisfy us men,
  Since we were young, my friend, since we were
    young.
Light thoughts of scented missives and the tender
    wiles of love,
Are banished with those younger years we're often
    dreaming of;
The eyes that captured with a glance, the lips that
    spoke our names,
Belong to plain old spinsters now or fat-and-forty
    dames!
And yet I doubt if riches, or if yet the bay that twines,
Bring half the joys to us grown "boys" who thought
    of valentines.

ON RAINY DAYS.

ON rainy days Care flings its goad away,
    And to the sway of Peace's influence yields;
The outside world grows holier, as the day
  Christ passed along among the Sabbath fields.
From out a copse a dove's mellifluous coo
  Blends with the softness of the blurry haze;
And drowsy chimney swallows sink from view,
    On rainy days.

All sounds are low and mellow like the tone
  Of some cathedral organ notes, the while
A sparrow twitters by its nest alone,
  And geese march through the lot in Indian file.
And from a cottage, on the air a-swim,
  A woman's voice swells in a song of praise,
And then my soul floats heavenward on the hymn,
    On rainy days.

THINK OF ME, LITTLE GIRL.

THOU art nearing the time all too fast, little girl,
　　When womanly yearning shall wake;
May the talisman, hope, linger well to the last,
　And shield thee from tears and heartbreak!
Though thy dreams to the least be entirely fulfilled,
And thy burgeoning faith-buds be never once chilled,
Still turn from thy dreams in the joyful whirl,
And think of me once in a while, little girl.

Womanhood's coming apace, little girl,
　With promise of visions so sweet;
And Love that is tender will seek thy embrace,
　And his glances thy pure ones will greet.
One lonely old bosom will oftentimes ache,
Though I show thee but smiles for thy dear little sake;
Then turn from thy dreams in the everyday whirl,
To think of me once in a while, little girl!

IN THE SHADE.

LEANING upon the shaded fence, I feel
    A sense of keen enjoyment through me steal;
I live alone in the ideal and dream,
And all things with a floating vagueness gleam;
Strange pageants seem to fill the morning air,
And music rises from I know not where.

The bees, as lovers' mouths on loved ones' lips,
Cling to the blooms whence dewy nectar drips;
Bell-tinklings, mellowed by the distance, fall
Like stray refrains from over Heaven's wall;
And meadows spread in sun and shade away,
Inviting Pan to hereward come and stay.

ROBERT BURNS.

A HAMELY lot was thine, Bob Burns—ane filled
    wi' mickle t'il;
Yet e'en for thee the mavis sang an' gowans lo'ed to
    smile.
An' a' the warld is glad to-day to claim thee as its ain,
An wad noo, shouldst thou ask for it, gie bread an' not
    a stane!
        Thy fame is ower a' the earth,
           Each heart to thine ain turns:
        Nae ither bard's poetic worth
           Maun shadow thine, Bob Burns.

Our love is like thine ain, Bob Burns, for her thy heart
    held dear—
"Time but the impression deeper makes" as "channels
    deeper wear!"
Though born unknown 'mang Scotia's braes, we gie to
    thee to-day

The honors that we gie the great—that ne'er maun dee
    awa'!
        Thy fame is ower a' the earth,
          Each heart to thine ain turns:
        Nae ither bard's poetic worth
          Maun shadow thine, Bob Burns.

UNDER THE FRESH GREEN GRASS.

LOVE and affection for some, and existence perennial May;
Yearning in vain for others as the seasons go on their
   way;
But all of it finds surcease, the laughter as well as the
   sighs,
Under the fresh green grass, under the old blue skies.

Greatness and glory for some, and the tribute of praise
   and song;
Obscurity alone for others "as long as life—as long;"
Yet glory shall nothing avail, no matter what fame de-
   nies,
Under the fresh green grass, under the old blue skies.

Heaven's not bought with a price, and earth's not
   holden in fee;
And leveled are caste and degrees far over the jasper
   sea;
But sweet shall the slumbering be of happy and tearful
   eyes,
Under the fresh green grass, under the old blue skies.

INGERSOLL.

THROUGH the land has sped the message that
the infidel is dead—

Gone the power of verbal magic; low the one-time
proud-poised head.

Even the believer pauses and expresses genuine ruth

For the death of one whose genius might have been
a lamp for youth,

Who yet followed Doubt—regarding it the harbinger
of Truth.

There are few whose faith he sneered at will contest
the praise, Love-made,

That he, dealing with his fellows, noble attributes dis-
played.

Charity—which Christ exalted when upon the earth—
is fain

To admit the friendly tribute, though the questions
still remain:

What have men gained by his talents? What in scof-
fing did he gain?

Doubt—the agent of the Dark One—may the stout-
    est hearts assail:
Is it best to yield—and suffer, when a bold front may
    avail?
There before him glowed the record: *Men have heark-
    ened to the Word,*
And have heaved the old world Godward, while within
    their bosoms stirred
A sweet hope that surges bravely and in death is not de-
    terred!

Was there wisdom in assuming that a mortal has the
    right
To destroy the day—then give us naught but darkness
    for the light?
Was it wise to view the deathbed, where the dying are
    made glad,
Or the progress of the peoples who the Christian hope
    have had,
Then declare their creeds pernicious and their votaries
    but mad?

Men are weak; the way is stony; and we stumble on
    the road:
None may rightly judge their struggles where no eye
    can see the load.
But Jehovah's mercy's boundless, and its reach none
    hath divined—
Let us trust some Christian's prayers in the days that
    lie behind
Have availed somewhat the scoffer as he plodded on
    doubt-blind.

THE STARS.

I.

TWAS eve in Bethlehem, the while the spheres
Were younger yet by many hundred years.

The crowded town was fluttering in unrest,
Filled well with those who came to be assessed.

There were the bearded patriarchs from the hills
Beyond where Jordan its low music trills;

Young maidens in their beauty darkly fair;
The aged, and the newly wedded pair.

The soft eyes of the wondering children gazed
On stolid camels, pleased or half-amazed;

And peasants—simple for the lives they led—
Watched how King Herod's soldiers kept their tread,

And thought, perhaps, of other cycles when
Judea had her strong, courageous men.

Beyond the city limits sunshine spread
About each lonely peak a hood of red,

And round their rugged base, footpathed and brown,
The gathering shadows wove a somber gown.

From where the flocks browsed in their far retreat,
Came some rude shepherd's anthem, tender-sweet,

While pleasing as where toppling censers spill,
Arose the fragrance of the yellow dill.

At last the twilight; then the darkness; then
The star that told the Saviour's birth to men.

II.

A later day now flushed Judea's land;
But while the dawn shone bright from strand to strand,

Men's hearts were sore, believing Death had won
A victory o'er the Lord's anointed One.

Fair lay the barley fields; the cumin bloomed;
Far-off the cross on bald Golgotha loomed;

The camels with their bearded riders strode
With swinging gait along the dusty road;

The almond blossoms, as a pictured psalm,
Were blended with the foliage of the palm;

THE STARS.

The voice of children sounded on the ear
As soft as hymns from a diviner sphere;

Mailed sentinels stood drowsing by the gates,
Grim as the minions of the frowning Fates.

But suddenly the world was thrilled, and far
A halo mantled vale and mountain scar;

An Unseen Hand reached through the morning's stir,
Unwinding graveclothes in the sepulcher;

And from the opened tomb there came to sight
The deathless Harbinger of Hope and Light;

And "Christ is risen!" hymned the choir divine,
As rose the Star that shall forever shine!

A LULLABY.

SWEET an' low, sof' an' low,
   An' sweetly as de rivah's flow,
We heahs de music cross de sea
Whah spreads de lan' ob Is-ter-Be.
   An' sweet an' low, an' sof' an' low,
   De baby's teensy footfalls go;
But bimeby he's gwine be at peace
   Whah roses spring an' lilies blow.

De music comes f'om hahps ob gol',
Tetched by de fingers nevah ole,
An' Gawd leans down, leans down to heah
De strains dat's floatin' to His eah.
   An' sweet an' low, an' sof' an' low,
   De baby's teensy footfalls go;
But bimeby he's gwine be at peace
   Whah roses spring an' lilies blow.

NIGHT IN THE CITY.

THE shadows of night-time grope
    From dens somewhere in the skies;
The eyes of the city ope
    And look on night in surprise,
Staring with batless glare from the mortared monsters
    there.

Far off—giant glowworms—crawl
    The cars through the restless marts;
The chimes from the churches fall
    Like hammers on felons' hearts;
While a moment side by side a harlot and virgin glide.

At last, as the hours grow late,
    The servants of slumber creep;
Then stalketh Sin in his hate
    Where the pure and innocent sleep:
Has God placed on doorposts there a signet that crime
    must spare?

123

UNC' CÆSAR'S PHILOSOPHY.

UNC' CÆSAR made money an' frien's an' sich like,
    Though he nevah made effort to be no big Ike;
An' I axed how to prospah lak' him, when de frown
Ob bad luck seemed hovahrin' always aroun';
An' he ses, wid a smile an' a voice monst'ous strong:
"Hol' a stiff uppah lip an' dess go right erlong."

A niggah's expression, an' it's homely, you'll say,
But it's troof widout furbelo's an' sich, anyway.
It means grit an' melt, an' a will foh to do,
An' a heaht dat don't shirk at no small bugaboo!
It's a mighty good sayin', ef coa'se. foh a song:
"Hol' a stiff uppah lip an' dess go right erlong!"

LEN.

(A Memory.)

WE knew him by the name of Len,
And none could tell precisely when
His surname was the last time called
Within the village, mountain-walled,
And sleeping like a hound at ease
Beneath blue skies and locust trees.
He truant played at ev'ry school,
And "You will live your days a fool,"
His father said when naught could make
The son the narrow pathway take.
The years went by, and while there died
Full many through the country side,
He seemed to linger year by year.
  Men said the fellow was so low
That Death just gave to him a sneer,
  And, passing by, would let him go!

He saw the homestead going down
That once enhanced the little town;

LEN.

The hollyhocks his mother loved—
 He saw them choked by alien weeds;
The orchard path which he had roved
 Grew noisome with the swaying reeds;
The catbirds, which had loved to sing
In many a dead and vanished spring,
Seemed now disposed the place to shun
Where lizards loitered in the sun;
The nightshade twined about the door,
 Where oft his mother sat and sung,
When love for him was strong as pure,
 And hope some rays about him flung;
The spiders hung their nets around;
 Across the bare floor hopped the toad;
And what seemed once as holy ground,
 Was desolation's own abode.

If Len e'er noticed this, I think
 No sigh would melt and run in tears.
He drank when men would give him drink,
 Nor rendered heed to passing years.
But somehow all the children seemed
To love him, and their wee eyes beamed

With childish glee when he would romp
With them at twilight as the pomp
Of spring or summertime made sweet
With fragrant blooms the village street.
He lived within an alley dark,
 And there one winter night I passed.
Far off, the watchdog's lonely bark;
 Above, the skies with clouds o'ercast;
And as I paused beside his door,
I saw him sitting, bending o'er
The brushwood fire, whose timid glow
Sent shadows dancing to and fro.
His face was resting on his hand,
His hair uncombed and straggling, and
He hummed a few words of a strain—
Hummed and rehummed them o'er again:

"Clasped to your heart
 In a loving embrace,
With your light lashes
 Just sweeping your face,
Never hereafter

127

To wake or to weep—
Rock me to sleep, mother,
Rock me to sleep!"

That night the greatest snowstorm known
  Came whitely shrouding field and fen,
And winds rushed by with fearful moan
  And startled every hill and glen;
And, late, I heard a cry of fright
  From one whose six-year lad was lost.
He'd tried to cross the street that night
  While homeward bound, but soon was tossed
A victim to the storm fiend's will,
Which boded for all creatures ill!

We searched the village everywhere;
Then, giving up in our despair,
We turned our footsteps home once more,
When faintly through the gusty roar
We heard a low and wailing sound;
And thus the lad—and Len—were found!
The boy was safe, and round him thrown
  The tattered coat that Len had doffed;

But from the man the breath had flown—
   "The wreck" that we had often scoffed;
He'd heard the little wand'rer's cry,
And, for his sake, went out to die.

Who knows but this old world is less
Borne down with woe and bitterness
For those whose lives to our eyes seem
Unworthy even faint esteem?
So there were many tears shed when
The poor old form was hid from men;
And somehow we all like to say
   That one who loved the children so,
   Was bound some noble traits to know—
And Christ, . . . perhaps He thinks that way.

A DISAPPOINTED FELLOW.

OF course I'm sour—I've a right to be;
    How much has been denied me in this world!
In the first place, I did not get to see
    Fair Eden and the streams that therein swirled.

I'm truly sorry that I never viewed
    Queen Cleopatra in her perfect flower;
Nor sat with Homer when in pleasant mood,
    And heard him chatting for, say, one brief hour.

I might have gained an autograph from Paul,
    Made pictures of young Saul and David each;
Or maybe heard Mark Antony when the fall
    Of Cæsar roused that big spread-eagle speech.

I might have seen St. John when tempest tossed,
    Or heard from living lips sweet Sappho's lays;
And then—but, brooding over what I've lost,
    I'm sure I shall go sighing all my days!

THE SYMBOL STARS.

I STOOD on a peak where the starlight
   Shone as signals away and away, . . .
Till each far light failed, and each far light
   Disappeared in the dazzle of day.

And I thought while I tarried dumb there—
   As the stars are but lost in the light,
In the glorious glare of God's Somewhere
   Live our loved that are hidden from sight.

131

JUSTICE.

THE sweetest warbler he is called—
   The mockbird of our sylvan ways;
And yet he borrows all his strains
   From birds whose notes we rarely praise.

And many a song by masters sung,
   Whose strength and music we revere,
Was first suggested by some one
   Whose minor notes men failed to hear.

JAMES WHITCOMB RILEY.

SOME may praise the lines of Milton, some conceits
    of Keats recall,
  But I love the human feeling that from Riley's lyre
    rings;
And the "poet of the cornfields" will one day be
    crowned by all
  As the master God inspired to make us love—the
    lowlier things.

QUATRAINS.

SPRING.

THE year is but a volume God has penned
    Whose lays the passing season's breezes sing;
Its sweetest thoughts, from opening to the end,
    Are the first blossoms of the poem, Spring.

FRIENDS.

Though we are worn and weary from some loss,
    Yet on life's journey many friends there be—
The Simons who assist to bear the cross
    Along the stony road to Calvary.

THE CHILDREN.

God help us prize the little ones we have,
    And realize in time our blessing's worth;
For every passing moment is a wave
    That bears them farther from our arms and hearth.

ASSISTANCE.

A near-by oak, uprooted by the storms,
  Yet leans upon an elm, and leaves and seeds;
As some ruined life, upheld by kindly arms,
  Is spared to bloom awhile in noble deeds.

SUNSET.

Flushed as from racing over vales and streams,
  He disappears as though from light and life;
The sun before the moon a Joseph seems
  Who flees from Potiphar's enamored wife.

THE CAUSE OF CUBA.

(1896.)

I.

THE Cubans will yet be beaten? Their cause can
    never be won?
  But Right will never stay beaten, and its hopes will
    broaden, I ween;
For out in the limitless future, as plain as the conquer-
    less sun,
  The spirit of Freedom rests couchant—unawed, un-
    frightened, serene!

II.

Xerxes with chains on the sea, and his lackeys there
    with their knouts—
  Tyrannous, purpled and proud as he sits on his
    throne on the shore;
While with only a heave of the breast, as it tosses gray
    mane and shouts,
  His "victim" can scatter his fleet and shatter a thou-
    sand more!

III.

And lives there a regent to-day whom cruelty's vices al-
    lure,
  Who thinks that in this God's age of yearning and
    manhood brave,
He can shackle a people for aye and they will the chains
    endure?
  They will rise in their might and strike till they've
    driven him to his grave!

IV.

Warm as the current that flows with the Mexic gulf's
    warm stream,
  And clear as the rivulets were that murmured
    through Eden's ways,
There runneth a deathless purpose, which, beautiful as
    a dream,
  Will drown cold Tyranny's hordes and Tyranny's
    strongholds raze!

V.

The Cubans will yet be beaten? Their cause can never
    be won?

But Right will never stay beaten, and its hopes will
broaden, I ween;
For out in the limitless future, as plain as the conquer-
less sun,
The spirit of Freedom rests couchant—unawed, un-
frightened, serene!

A HOPE.

WHAT man will say: "He sought me in the strife,
　　And bathed my wounds when men deserted
　me?"
What heart have I made lighter in my life,
　Though God knows I have loved humanity?
And yet this hope still lightens much of pain—
Who hath endeavored hath not lived in vain!

PARTING.

WHERE the white road the mountain's coarse
    hair parted,
  Spilled nectar, but a moment sunshine flowed;
The whippoorwills their night-long chansons started,
  And on the sky cloud tents of Bedouins glowed.

Two stood beside the farmhouse gate—a maiden,
  And he who there with Hope's misguiding eyes
Saw fame ahead, as some child legend laden
  Believes beyond the rainbow treasure lies.

They stood a moment there, while the insistent
  Drone of the insects welled up mellowly;
And then two paths, that ever grew more distant,
  Were blazed out by the murmured word "Good-by."

BEYOND RECALL.

SUNBEAMS love to shimmer
  'Mong the summer ways,
But to my eyes dimmer
  Are the golden rays.
Hope's fair hands are folden,
  Love is sleeping low
In the olden, golden
  Days of Long Ago.

Matters not the falling
  Of your bitter tears;
To my heart are calling
  Yearnings through the years—
Voices ere were folden
  Hands so fair to me
In the golden, olden
  Days of Use-to-Be.

Maybe had your bosom
　　Learned with truth to thrill,
Sweets of bud and blossom
　　Had existed still;
Hands had not been folden,
　　Love not sleeping low
In the olden, golden
　　Days of Long Ago.

I've the vine's defection,
　　You the fruitless tree:
Mine the recollection,
　　Yours the memory:
And, for both, hands folden
　　That were fair to see,
In the golden, olden
　　Days of Used-to-Be.

ANTIPODES.

I.

A MOTHER'S eyes and a trusting child—
  A babe in its innocence given;
And Christ might say with his manner mild:
  "Of such is the kingdom of heaven."

II.

A siren's voice and a youth's weak will,
  And vice that all manhood effaces;
Then over the gulf in her kisses' thrill,
  And to hell in a woman's embraces!

REMORSE.

ALONE in her room with the pitiless foe
 Of thought that never will sleep, it seems—
Whispering hints of the long ago
  And the dear dead dreams!

The clock ticks on as it has for an age;
  Her Herrick is oped on the étagère;
And the whole place seems but a poet's page
  In praise of her.

Her portrait is looking down from the wall—
  Her eyes aglow with the pure sweet light,
As the stargleams over the pathway fall
  Of a man at night. .   .   .

You have your revenge at last, at last,
  O sweet lost love of the old lost years!
For joy is a wreck in the sea of the past,
  And submerged in tears!

HAGAR.

I.

HARD by the fountain in the way to Shur
    Hagar the outcast tarried in her woe.
The breeze was sullen—no refreshing stir
    Arose among the leaves; the sun's hot glow
    Fell scorching over hill and valley low;
Like fallen women drooped the wayside flowers,
    Worn out by their depleting passion's flow;
And slowly, slowly passed the hot-breathed hours,
As though old Joshua were near to test his powers!

II.

A swarthy beauty shone about her face,
    Such as still clings around the rose that's thrown
Downward from where awhile 'twas wont to grace
    Some maiden's pure and palpitating zone.
    The way that led from Kadesh was how lone,
As though there Silence stalked with muffled feet,
    Save once a bird (a fleck of cadence blown
From some fair tropic clime, divinely sweet)
Let melt its melody to charm the weird retreat.

10   145

III.

"O, but to die!" she thought, while far above
  A vulture, like a bark on Galilee,
Poised dark and seeming moveless. "Dreaming of
  The being that I was and now must be,
  Eats out my helpless heart!. Lord, pity me!"
And ere her prayers had ceased there came a sound
  Of rustling pinions, making cadency;
The while an angel's fingers healed the wound
That ached within her heart, and heaven beamed
    around.

IV.

The centuries have passed since those far days,
  And time has grayer grown; the cold white moon
Still casts her polished lances down the ways
  As in the nights gone by; the almonds swoon
  Along the roadways, and the bulbuls croon;
While Hagar's dust is lost, or watched by none   -
  Save God who loved her. But, athrill, atune,
Still ring those musicked glances that outshone
From God's eyes when he heard a helpless outcast's
    moan!

146

DOWN ON THE FARM—A MEDLEY.

PROEM.

SOME gleams of sunshine in rhyme's thrall,
  Some hints of old ways meshed in song—
These all I bring, my little all,
  To catch the notice of the throng.

How trivial and how tame!   And still—
  Though all of grace and art I lack—
Some unforgetting heart may thrill
  To have them even thus brought back.

I.

At times 'tis all monotonous, you too are prone to say?
The same old hills in sun and shade, the same folks
    day by day?
And you are almost led to think the very whippoorwill
I heard when but a youngster calls from out the thicket
    still?   .   .   .
God made the country; man, the town—a worn-out
    song again!
But then I've tried them both, and would not modify
    the strain.

II.

A stroll up the road, on the still spring days,
That winds with the creek through the pastoral ways!
The kingfisher, stretching its blue neck, flies
Through interlaced shadows with startled cries;
In the rail fence corners the wild rose gleams
Pink as old loves' lips come back in our dreams;
On the sloping hillsides cattle drowsily laze;
  And we think of "still waters"
   In the Land that is fadeless
    On still spring days.

God is loving the world when he sends spring days
By the sun-catching streams—to the emerald ways!
The smell of the hay from the meadow comes in;
Mellowed to song blade and whetrock's din;
The miracle of fishes and loaves is outdone
In this feast for the senses of every one;
And I think, when my soul from its tenement strays,
  'Twill long to pass hereward
   On its outbound journey
    On still spring days.

III.

The hours in the deep summer ways
 Go to sleep in a bed of blooms;
 While Faith like a David looms
O'er the prostrate form of Doubt, and your spirit lifts
 up its praise.
  Regret, as a sad dream flees
  When the morning's eyes ope wide,
  Floats out on a passing tide
Till faint as the hint of a sail far out on the twilight
 seas.

  The scents from the forestside drift
  Serenely to you, as a gift
In a chalice of tropical winds blown onward and on
 and on;
  While you feel in the roses' smell
  Lie mummies of dreams that tell
Of the hopes that were sweet and dear in the dear
 sweet years long gone.

  Except for the dissonant cries
  Of the jay on the sun-loved hill—

Rustling the silence as sighs
Of a nun vibrating her veil in her love for a lost love
    still—
    There's peace in the runnel clear,
      And rest with contented herds;
      Yea, joy in the flutter of birds;
And you know in the reigning peace and the beauty
    the Lord is near!

IV.

I think when God looks downward on the autumn
    scenes unfurled
He feels fresh satisfaction in the beauty of His world!
True, flower scents are scarcer than in leafy days of
    June,
And bird-songs are more plaintive than some summer
    afternoon;
There's something in the quiet, though, as sweet as
    sweetest rhymes—
The Still Small Voice is nearer then than at all other
    times.
The crickets, like wee carriers that whistle where
    they go,

Bring tender little messages from those we used to
    know;
We journey through the gate unlatched by Fancy's
    servitor,
To where we had our sweetest dreams and where the
    old friends are,
And halfway wish that life had passed with all our
    boyish dreams,
When ripened nuts are falling with a spatter in the
    streams.

V.

On winter nights we learn the truth, when by the fire
    alone,
That day thoughts are not such as those that come
    when day is flown.
The clock's tick on the mantelpiece may be the only
    voice
Now left to call to mind the tones that made us once
    rejoice,
And features so familiar then, and smiles that we re-
    call,
Are passed away or live alone in pictures on the wall.

VI.

And over at the graveyard, where my little firstborn
    lies—
He'd be well grown and manly now—the mockbird's
    warblings rise.
'Tis strange none talk about him when the catbird
    pipes at dawn,
For still he's with me all the time, as in the decades
    gone.
I wish that I could look on him just like he used to be,
A chubby little fellow still and toddling after me;
I wish that I could hear him once yet shouting at his
    play
As ere the angels, coming down, decoyed my boy
    away.
At nights when he grew weary he would climb upon
    my knees,
And, nestling cheek against my cheek, plead: "Yist
    one stowey, p'ease!"
Although it seems but childish to recall such little
    things,
His prattle, innocent and dear, in recollection rings.

So many things go out of life that we had learned to
    prize,
And leave an ashen heap alone to mark Time's sacri-
    fice;
But saddest is the passing of the baby words that die
With childhood and are heard no more save in the
    memory.
Friends' comfortings can warm no more than star-
    fires in the night;
Philosophy's a feeble thing when Grief leaps up in
    might!
But clearer than the voice of youth, ere youth be over-
    past,
The song his mother used to sing of peace that comes
    at last:

VII.

"Far out through the mists of the Now, in the lily-
    loved region of Then,
    Are the hills of One of these Days;
The lights and the shadows lie soft as sleep in the
    overworked eyes of men,
    On the hills of One of these Days.

The noon is as deathless as truth and love; unheard
    is the sound of *no more;*
The music of lutes rings hopefully out, responding to
    Joy's encore,
Now full on the ears entranced, now faint on the
    tropical shore,
        And the hills of One of these Days,
        The hills of One of these Days.

God fashioned them out of the loss of the pleasures
    of Paradise—
        The hills of One of these Days—
To gladden the spirit that tires of the world with its
    tears and its tearful good-bys,
        The hills of One of these Days.
O, fresh as the smile of a friend, when the patience of
    hearts seems vain;
As bright as a steadfast splendor aglow in the midst
    of the rain;
And dear as the eyes we have loved, come back in a
    dream again,
        Are the hills of One of these Days,
        The hills of One of these Days!"

VIII.

But hold! . . . The ruralite, you know, is not
    obliged to sit

In solitude and never note men's wisdom and their
    wit.

I've marked lines in my Shakespeare, and I dote on
    Milton, too;

I'reserve my Homer from the dust, keep Dante bright
    and new,

To be prepared should some guest speak about the
    poets old,

Who hid in many-worded quartz their grains of pre-
    cious gold!

Let me confess—when fain to spend an hour from
    worldly smart,

Like Longfellow then I seek some one whose songs
    gushed from his heart.

O yes; I like my Shakespeare much, and Milton's
    lines, indeed;

I keep great poems but to praise, the minor ones to
    read! . . .

But poetry is giving way to the Commercial Age,

And sentiment will be no more our cherished heritage?

Well, Mammon is a selfish king, oppressing where he may,

But God's curse follows him—the heart will yet dispute his sway!

IX.

Mammon's forces for a while may drive the patient sons of men,

Laugh to scorn the social prophet with a future-probing ken;

But the masses, turned to vassals by the Pharaohs on the throne,

Finding that their tasks are doubled should they murmur or make moan,

Will yet prove the past has really settled one eternal truth:

That the power that sows oppression in the end must garner ruth!

Anarchy? Let that be throttled! Liberty? Let that be hailed

As the friend of law and progress, unimpeached and
    unassailed!
But the Czar is not a despot that we have the most
    to fear;
Mammon hath the eyes that see not and the ears that
    will not hear;
And old sentiment, long-suffering, knows that it is not
    decreed
That those made in Deity's likeness must forever bow
    to greed!

When the masses rise like Samson, trying if their
    strength be shorn;
Feeling through their pulses quiver the fresh energy
    of morn;
Brooding on the wrongs of ages, trembling in their
    new-roused hate;
Fiercer for the wakened devil rushing through the
    patience gate—
What shall be the end, O dreamer? What disasters
    dire will swarm
When the thongs that bound fall broken and the
    masses lift their arm?

X.

But pessimism is a plant whose blossom is distress;
Be mine to make hope more and more, and doubt for-
    ever less.
By looking we may see a rose: and, listening, hear a
    song;
So let us trust the good in man may linger with us
    long. . . .
With thoughts that love best other days, and but a
    fossil now,
Few care, I think, when death may place his signet on
    my brow,
And yet I trust the time will be, when called on to
    depart,
While memories, as flowers in bloom, are fresh within
    my heart.

XI.

Out from the earthly harbor how soon will the go-
    ing be?
Will the sunbeams' play on the waters enjewel the
    smiling sea?

Will the moments be woeful or pleasant, will the voy-
    age be gloomy or gay,
On a course where the ship prows ever are headed the
    other way?
Shall we pass by the isles that are fragrant with flowers
    of a tropical clime,
Our bark with the blue waves moving as sweetly as
    rhyme with rhyme?

Out from the earthly harbor what time will the ship
    set sail?
Will the nights be formed of the shadows from wings
    of an endless gale?
Shall we crouch in our berths in silence while away
    on the desolate waste
Lost shallops go floundering helmless in a gloom that
    shall not be effaced?
Shall we pass near the mystical star lands where those
    of the other spheres
May shout in an unknown jargon their queries within
    our ears?

Out from the earthly harbor shall we drift in the by
and by,
Unnoticed the clinging of loved ones, unheeded the
kiss and the sigh.
But the compass of faith will avail us, and the prayers
that we have prayed
Will twinkle as lights in the distance, illuming the
heaviest shade;
And instead of the bell buoys sounding a warning of
ambushed harm,
We will hear, "It is I," from the Saviour, as He called
once before through the storm!